THE CATS OF CUCKOO SQUARE

THE CATS OF CUCKOO SQUARE

Two Stories

Adèle Geras

Illustrated by

Tony Ross

Delacorte Press

Published by
Delacorte Press
an imprint of
Random House Children's Books
a division of Random House, Inc.
1540 Broadway
New York, New York 10036

Text copyright © 1997 by Adèle Geras
Illustrations copyright © 1997 by Tony Ross

Visit us on the Web! www.randomhouse.com/kids
Educators and librarians, for a variety of teaching tools, visit us at
www.randomhouse.com/teachers

Cataloging-in-Publication Data is available from the Library of Congress.
ISBN: 0-385-72926-X

The text of this book is set in 18.5-point Bembo Schoolbook.
Book design by Trish P. Watts
Manufactured in the United States of America
October 2001
10 9 8 7 6 5 4 3 2 1
BVG

Contents

Blossom's Revenge

1. Prissy Arrives   9
2. From Bad to Worse   33
3. The Ghost-Cat   45
4. The Last Straw   71
5. Goodbye, Prissy!   81

Picasso Perkins

1. The Painting Competition   101
2. Hiding from Lexie   122
3. Posing for the Portrait   132
4. In the Studio   152
5. A Change of Plan   177
6. Fame!   184

Blossom's Revenge

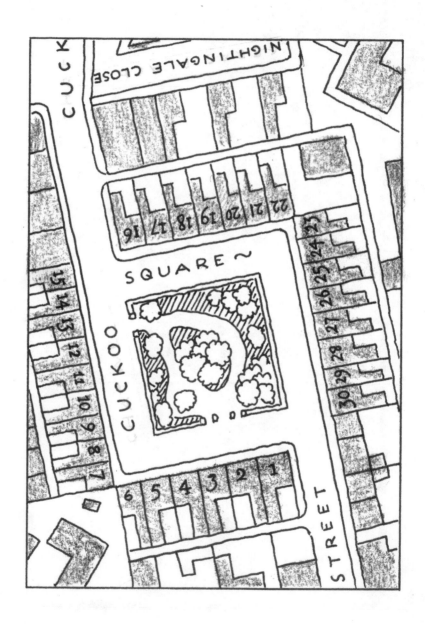

1.

Prissy Arrives

"Look at that cat!" said Prissy Pinkerton. "Why is it so fat?"

Honestly! I had never been so insulted in my life! I may not be as slim as I once was, but no one could possibly call me fat!

Prissy Pinkerton is a very nasty little girl. She doesn't look nasty. If you could see her, you would almost

certainly say "How sweet!" She is six
years old. She has curly golden hair.
She wears white socks. She sucks her
thumb. Her cheeks are dimpled. Her
eyes are blue. Nevertheless, she is
nasty. I knew she was nasty the
moment she opened her mouth to
speak.

My name is Blossom and I'm one
of the Cuckoo Square Cats. There's
a garden in the square, with railings
all around it and a gate that's kept
locked. The flower beds are well dug,
and there are plenty of shrubs under
whose branches we can hide. We like
sharpening our claws on the trees,
although it is only young kittens
who go scrabbling up to the
topmost branches just for the fun of
it. My friends and I are too old for
that sort of behavior. We sit on the

benches or flop about on the soft grass in the summer. The humans have keys to what we cats call Our Place, because we are the ones who use it most often.

My particular friends are Perkins (whose people are the Blythes at number 27), Callie (from number 18), and Geejay (whose real name is Ginger Jack, and who curls up in front of the fire at number 2). Perkins is a large, dignified tabby who has lived in the square longer than any of us,

Callie is a sweet-
natured, gentle calico
cat with white fur
prettily spotted in
orange and
black, and Geejay looks like a lion.
He has yellow eyes and is the best
hunter in the square.

As for me, I'm fluffy and black
and white, and I like to go through
life as calmly and peacefully
as I can.

Other cats come and go, and we allow them to walk through the square, but only on their way to somewhere else. This is our territory. This is where we come to get away from our humans, to exchange news, and especially to tell stories.

Earlier today, we were all waiting for the Pinkertons to arrive at my house with their little daughter.

"She is a relation," I told them. "Her name is Prissy. Her parents are bringing her to stay with us for the summer holidays while they find a new house and get it ready. She's supposed to be company for Miles."

Perkins opened one eye and announced, "Visitors never turn out to be what you think. We have them all the time." He yawned. "Wake me up when she arrives. I do not like to miss anything, but it is hard to keep one's eyes open."

"Perhaps," Callie murmured, "she'll be a lovely little girl."

Callie expects the best of everyone.

I, also, thought it would be delightful to have another child in our house. My people are called Mr. and Mrs. Randall, but I call them Mum and Dad because that is Miles's name for them. They are good humans,

although they have their faults.
Mum is house-proud. She prowls
through rooms armed with a
fearsome device called a Hoover,
which sucks dirt out of the carpet
and makes a most distressing noise.

When I was a kitten, I thought
the Hoover was a monster and hid
from it under the chest of drawers,
but I'm used to it now. Mum has a
long metal tube that she attaches to
the Hoover sometimes.
"This is my Dustbuster,
Blossom," she told me
once. "It works
wonders with
cat hairs."

Whenever Mum mentions cat
hairs, I yawn. She goes on and on
about them. They are her favorite
subject. She ought to be grateful

that I am black and white. I leave
pale hairs on the dark things and
dark hairs on the pale things, and
this allows her to play happily with
her Dustbuster almost every day.

Dad is a little absentminded.
Sometimes he doesn't notice me.
He has sat on me, tripped over me,
and even driven off in his car while
I was curled up asleep on the hood.

"He likes you when he *does* see you," Miles tells me, and I'm sure that's true, but Dad's mind is often on other things. Also, he wears glasses, which are supposed to help him to see better, but sometimes he puts them down and forgets where they are.

It is Miles who is my special friend. He is eight years old and he loves me. I know, because he tells me so. I wish I could have a sardine for every time he's said, "You're our best and most beautiful Blossom in the world."

When the Randalls talked about their niece, Prissy, I thought, "What a silly name!"

It turned out to be short for

Priscilla, but that didn't make it any better.

"Why does she have to come here?" Miles asked at breakfast one day.

"Well," said Mum, "Iris *is* my sister, and blood is thicker than water."

"What does that mean?" Miles asked.

"It means," said Dad gloomily, "that our lives are going to be turned upside down."

"Nonsense!" said Mum. "She's only six. What could she possibly do?"

I told the Cuckoo Square Cats what Mum had said as we waited for the Pinkertons' car.

Perkins sighed. "In my experience," he said, licking his left front paw, "the younger the child, the more things it finds to do, not all of them pleasant, I assure you."

"Look!" said Geejay, who was perched on the lowest branch of a tree. "Here comes a car I've never seen before. Is it them?"

"These humans go so fast," said Callie. "I wish they wouldn't. It gets my fur in a flurry."

I peered out from between the railings. A car was indeed coming up to the Randalls' front door, looking and sounding like some roaring, glittering beast. Three people got out of it and went up the steps to my house. One of them was a little girl.

"I shall go and introduce myself," I said to my friends. "It's good manners."

"She looks so pretty!" said Callie.

She did, but, as I have already said, her very first words made me realize how unkind she really was.

After saying I was fat she went on, "I *hate* fat cats!"

In my opinion, it's extremely impolite to say you hate a fellow creature.

"At least," I said to my friends, "Miles loves me exactly as I am."

And it's true. "We'd never swap you," he tells me, "for any scrawny, skinny, mangy old *thin* cat . . . you're our Blossom Butterball. You're beautiful."

I try to be modest about it, but it *is* true that in my younger days, everyone who saw me said I was a splendid creature. I am proud of my eyes, which are like green jewels: emeralds, perhaps, or clear, pale jade.

I crept around everyone's legs and waited for Mum and Dad to open the door. There was much squawking and kissing and shouts of "Iris!" and "Darling!" and "How lovely!" and "Prissy, how sweet you look!" I have never understood why humans make such a to-do about greeting one another. A great deal of time could be saved if they simply touched noses from time to time, as we do.

"Look!" said Prissy. "Flowers!" She
bent down to pick a geranium from
one of the big flowerpots (Mum's
pride and joy) standing beside the
front door.

I could see that Mum was not
pleased at all. She put her hand on
Prissy's shoulder and said, "Please
don't do that, dear. The flowers look
so pretty where they are. Come
inside and have a drink."

I don't think anyone but me
noticed how Prissy pressed her lips
together and narrowed her eyes. She
was obviously a child who liked her
own way.

"Come along, darling," her
mother said. "Let's get these suitcases
indoors."

Prissy seemed to have a lot of
luggage for a small child.

"I'll take these two," said Uncle
Cliff, Prissy's father.

"But I want to bring something!" said the dainty little thing, and I could see her bottom lip begin to tremble. Later, I learned that when Prissy said "I want," trouble was never very far away.

Uncle Cliff said, "Right, then. You bring in that small one."

I was behind Prissy and saw exactly what she did when no one was looking. The grown-ups had gone into the hall. Prissy picked up her suitcase and accidentally-on-purpose, as Miles would say, swung around so that a corner of the case knocked one of the flowerpots over. It went flying down the front steps, shattering into a thousand fragments and leaving bits of earth

and torn petals everywhere. Prissy
giggled and muttered something
under her breath.

I saw her satisfied smirk, but no
one else did. I stared at the child,
and she glared back at me. She had
certainly seen me looking at her.

"Go away, horrid cat!" she said. "I'm going to call my mummy and I know what I'm going to say." Then she yelled "Mummee!" so loudly that my fur stood on end. Her mother and father came out, closely followed by the Randalls.

"Oh, dear," said Auntie Iris. "Whatever happened?"

"That cat," said Prissy. "It scared me. It made me swing my case and then the pot got hit."

If there is one thing all cats hate, it is being called "it."

"Never worry, old sport," boomed Uncle Cliff. "We'll pay for the damage . . . good as new in no time, eh?"

"I'll get a broom," said Mum. She

was upset, I could see. "You all go in for a cup of tea."

I went back to Perkins, Callie, and Geejay, who had been watching the drama unfold.

"Did you see what she did?" I asked them. My fur was still standing on end from the injustice of it all. "She blamed *me*! How dare she?"

"That child," said Perkins, "is nothing but trouble, mark my words."

"Perhaps," said Callie, "it was just an accident."

"If that was an accident," said Geejay, "my tail's a feather duster!"

2.
From Bad to Worse

Prissy Pinkerton did not get better.
After her parents left, she got worse.

"They've given her my room,
Blossom," said Miles. "I've got to
sleep in the spare room. She's
allowed to play with all my stuff."

I rubbed my head against his
hand to express my sympathy. Prissy
had been upsetting me, too. It's a

tradition in the Randall house that we all sit down to breakfast together. There are four chairs around the kitchen table, one for each of the humans and one for me. I like listening to Dad reading snippets of news from the paper (if he hasn't lost his glasses), and Miles gives me his buttery knife to lick when Mum's back is turned. On her first morning in our house, Prissy came down to breakfast and took no notice of the extra chair Mum had brought in for her from the hall. I had been asleep, but opened one eye when Prissy came into the room. The next thing that happened felt to me like an earthquake.

"Off! Off, cat," she giggled, and

she tipped my chair violently
forward so that I slid to the floor in
a muddle, with my heart beating so
loudly from the dreadful shock that
I was surprised no one else could
hear it. I went off with my tail
swishing behind me to show how
angry I was and sat on the window
seat, wishing I was the sort of cat
who enjoys scratching people.

"That's Blossom's chair!" Miles was indignant.

"It's my chair now," said Prissy and sat down firmly. "Where's the apple juice?"

"There's orange juice or milk," Mum cooed soothingly.

"I want apple juice!" Prissy said.

"We'll get some when we go shopping. Have some cereal . . . here."

"I like Poppycrunch!"

"We haven't got Poppycrunch," said Mum. "We'll get some. We'll go to the shops straight after breakfast."

Prissy picked up a piece of toast and left the room nibbling it.

"Poor little thing!" said Mum to Dad. "I expect she's missing her parents."

When Mum and Miles and Prissy had left for the shops, I went into the square to see if my friends were in the garden. I found Callie stretched out under a hydrangea bush.

She opened one eye and said, "You don't look a bit happy, Blossom."

"I was tipped out of my chair this morning. That hasn't happened to

me for years. In the Randall house, cats have equal rights to chairs. No one would dream of tipping me off."

"Really?" said Callie. "That's very unusual, you know. Most humans remove cats from anything they want to sit on, though it's true there are ways and ways of doing it. Prissy could have picked you up kindly and settled you somewhere else. There was no need for tipping."

Later that afternoon, Prissy said to Miles, "Miles, play with me. I want to play."

"How nice, dear," said Mum. "Your cousin wants to play with you. I'll go and start supper."

She left the room, and Miles and

Prissy were alone—except for me, of course. I was curled up on my part of the sofa, wide awake, ears wide open but eyes half closed.

"Let's play princesses," said Prissy. "You can be my coachman, and"—she turned her twinkly little eyes on me—"you can be the royal pet and sit on this cushion."

"No, she can't," said Miles. "That's my mum's best cushion."

"I say she can," Prissy pouted, and she scooped me up, lifted me into the air, and was about to plonk me down on the cushion. I do not like being picked up. I am too old for it. I do not like playing games, either, so I wriggled out of her grasp. I admit my claws were out, and I

suppose I might *just* have snagged
Prissy's finger with one of them.

She dropped me to the floor and began to shriek. "Auntieee! It's scratched me! There's blood! Horrible cat! Bad cat! Shoo! Go away!" She aimed a kick at me, but I managed to slip behind the sofa.

"Oh, darling!" Mum said, running into the room. "What's Blossom done, then? Come on, Blossom, where are you hiding? This isn't a bit like you!"

You should have seen the fuss! The running around in search of Band-Aids! The fetching of antiseptic and cotton swabs! The tears! The sweets to stop the tears! It was almost suppertime when the scene was over, and by then Prissy no longer felt like playing princesses.

"I want to draw," she said. "I want to do a picture."

"Okay," said Miles. "You go up. I'm coming."

When she'd gone, he bent down to stroke me.

"It wasn't your fault, Blossom. She's awful."

I purred at him to show I agreed.

"Now I've got to go and watch her leaving the tops off my felt-tip pens." He sighed as he left the room.

3.
The Ghost-Cat

"I wish Prissy Pinkerton," I told the Cuckoo Square Cats, "would just go away. She is a thorough nuisance."

"Many children," said Perkins, "are nuisances. You should make yourself scarce. That's what I do. We have a shed in our garden that's most convenient for that purpose."

"But Miles likes to talk to me," I

said. "He and I know what Prissy is
really like. Mum and Dad keep
patting her on the head and telling
Miles to be kind to her, as she's
missing her parents. Last night, she
had Mum rushing up and down the
stairs for ages with glasses of water
and slices of apple, and this morning
a dreadful thing happened in the
bathroom."

"Tell us about it," said Callie. Geejay wasn't really listening. He had his eye on a squirrel under one of the benches.

"I sometimes have my morning snooze there," I said. "It has a particularly soft carpet. This morning I was asleep when that dreadful child Prissy came in to wash. I thought I was hidden behind the clothes basket, but she must have seen my tail peeping out, because she started talking to me."

"That's better than tipping you off chairs and shouting at you," said Callie.

"Not really," I told her. "Not when you hear what she said. She said, 'I can see you, fat cat, and I'm going to pay you back for scratching me. You watch.' I made myself as small as I could, curling up tight with my tail tucked well in. Prissy knelt down near the sink. 'Look, fat cat,' she said. 'You've sat on the toothpaste tube and squashed it because you're so fat, and now see the mess.'

"She squeezed the tube and
trailed sticky white stuff all over the
carpet. Then she shook out a
blizzard of talcum powder and said,
'And you spilled the powder, too.
You're a bad cat and I'm going to

tell on you.' She left the room, and I could hear her calling from the top of the stairs, 'Auntie! Blossom's messed up the bathroom. Come and see!'

"Mum has only to hear the word 'mess' and she's there in an instant.

"'Oh, Blossom,' she wailed when she saw the state of the carpet. 'What *has* got into you? Downstairs this minute. Go on. Go. I'm very cross with you.'

"I streaked past her legs as quickly as I could, but my paws were covered in talcum powder and I've spent ages trying to lick it off. Have you ever tasted it? I feel quite ill!"

"It's disgusting," said Perkins. "I recommend a cooling drink."

"I had one," I said. "I finished all the water in my bowl, but I'm a little peckish now."

I said goodbye to my friends and padded into the house, wondering which of the cans in my own little cupboard Mum would have opened for my lunch.

★

I was eating my lunch of Purrfect
Liver and Rabbit when Prissy came
into the utility room.

I still find it hard to believe what
she did next.

She bent down behind me and
pulled my tail, very hard. I yowled, I
admit it, and Miles came running in
from the kitchen.

"I never!" said Prissy. "I never pulled Blossom's tail."

"You did, didn't you?" Miles said. "I know you did."

"I never!" wailed Prissy.

"What's all that noise?" Mum said. "Come in here at once, Miles, and stop shouting at poor little Prissy."

"But, Mum," Miles said. "She pulled Blossom's tail."

"Nonsense," said Mum. "I'm sure she'd never do anything like that. She probably trod on it by accident. It's a very long and bushy tail."

Well, I was happy to hear that my tail was properly appreciated, but I was beginning to wonder whether Miles and I should teach Prissy a lesson.

After lunch, he said to me, "Don't worry, Blossom. I've got ever such a good idea. I'm going to tell Prissy a special story this afternoon. Make sure you come and hear it."

At about five o'clock, the children were sitting on the sofa watching TV.

"Have you ever heard the story,

Prissy," Miles said, "about the ghost that haunts this house?"

"Doesn't," said Prissy, but her mouth was hanging open.

"It does. Listen. Once upon a time, long ago before we started living here, there was this girl."

"What was she called?" Prissy wanted to know.

"Mary," said Miles. "She had a cat called Tom."

I didn't think they were the most exciting names he could have chosen, but they must have been the first ones that popped into his head. I don't think he was expecting Prissy to be asking questions.

"Stop asking me things and just listen," he said. "Mary was so horrid to her cat that he ran away and got run over by a car."

I shivered. This is the fate that we cats fear most.

"Anyway," Miles continued, "Tom's ghost comes back to this house whenever there's a girl here. It's looking for Mary, but it's not good at telling one girl from another, so it'll probably come and haunt you. It's white and terrifying

and it meows in a specially howly
and scary way, and all its fur sticks
out and its eyes glow in the dark
and what it does is, it waits till
you're in bed, then it jumps on top
of you and digs its claws into the
quilt."

"There's no such thing as ghosts,"
said Prissy, but she ran out of the
room looking very nervous.

"Right," said Miles when she'd gone. "You're going to be the ghost-cat of Cuckoo Square. Can you howl like a banshee?"

I spent the next hour or so in the square, where my friends were full of good advice about how to turn myself into a bloodcurdling phantom.

"I was quite a yowler and a howler in my youth," said Perkins. "Listen to this." The sound he made flattened my ears against my skull.

"I couldn't do that!" I said.

"You have to practice," said Perkins. "Try it."

So I opened my mouth as wide as I could, and the noise that came out didn't sound as embarrassing as it might have done. I was obviously a very quick learner.

"Well done!" said Perkins. "Do that a few times and you'll be splendid."

"But you must learn to move like a ghost-cat, too," said Geejay. "No use plodding about sedately."

I sniffed. "I do *not* plod," I said.

"No, no, of course not," said Geejay hastily. "But you must creep menacingly, like this. Look."

He stretched his body out to its full length, crouched very close to the ground, and slunk along among the bushes like a tiger.

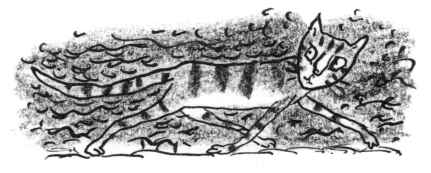

"I don't think," I said, "that the plumper sort of cat can manage to slink like that."

"I think you should try arching your back and spitting," Callie suggested. "That can be very scary sometimes."

Everyone agreed that arching my back suited me much better.

I was very pleased with myself. This acting seemed to be most enjoyable. "I'm quite looking forward to my performance," I said.

"What's that?" Prissy whispered, and sat up in bed. The shriek that came out of her mouth was much more banshee-like than anything I could have produced. I suppose I should have stopped there, but I was having fun. Leaping is something I only do in emergencies, because it is too much like hard work for the rounder type of cat. Still, I decided

★

That evening, as soon as Prissy was safely in her room, Miles came to find me. I would never have allowed anyone but him to dust me with flour, but I could see that to be a true ghost-cat, the whiter I was, the more terrifying I would be.

"You've got to be creepy," Miles told me. "Try to look ghostly."

Of course, Miles did not know that my friends had helped me and he was most impressed when I showed him what I could do.

"That's brilliant, Blossom. Really ace! Come on, now. We'll go and start."

I have to confess that I am perhaps a little too plump to be truly spooky, but I did my best. I crept into Prissy's room, where the curtains were closed. The first thing I did was arch my back and hiss a little.

to try to reach the bed for a little supernatural clawing of the quilt. I flung myself up as high as I could and landed next to Prissy's feet. She jumped out onto the floor and raced for the landing, leaving me a little out of breath.

"Auntiee!" she screeched. "Quick! The ghost-cat is here!"

Miles (who must have been peeping around the door) said, "Hide, Blossom! You were terrific, but we daren't let anyone see you now. Go on, behind the curtain."

I was sorry to leave the bed, but I understood that it would spoil our trick if Mum saw me. She'd know who I was, however much flour there was on my fur. No sooner was I safely out of sight than she came into the room, cuddling Prissy.

"Ghost-cat!" Prissy blubbered. "I saw the ghost-cat."

"There, there, lovey-chops," said Mum. "There's no such thing as a ghost-cat. You've had a bad dream.

I'll sing to you till you go to sleep again."

"Wasn't a dream," Prissy cried. "*Was* a ghost-cat. Miles told me."

"Miles, how could you?" Mum sighed. "Fancy making up the kind of story that would scare a little girl. It's very naughty of you. Go to bed at once. Go on."

Some time later, I pushed myself through the cat-flap and went to tell the Cuckoo Square Cats about the evening's adventures.

"Serves her right," said Geejay, when I'd finished my tale.

"An excellent prank!" Perkins agreed.

"I think you're very brave," said Callie. "I shouldn't like to have flour all over me."

"Miles brushed it off," I said. "Then I licked the bits he left behind. And I can tell you, it's not nearly as nasty tasting as talcum powder!"

4.
The Last Straw

The next day was Saturday. It was
very hot. The sun burned down from
the sky, and the Cuckoo Square
Cats were lying under the bushes,
looking as limp as kippers on a grill.

"I'm going home," I told them.
"I keep wanting to visit my water
bowl. Perhaps I shall come
out again after sunset."

"I would go home," said Perkins, "if only I could summon up the energy to cross the square."

I made my way to the patio and stretched myself out in a deep shadow. The stones were warm, and soon I was fast asleep. I was woken by someone's foot poking into my side. Miles and Mum and Dad would never prod a cat with their shoe. It was Prissy.

She bent down and said, "I know

it was you. You were the ghost-cat.
Auntie said. She found flour all over
the floor. So, yah boo and sucks to
you!"

She prodded me again and
wandered off. I should have run
away, but the thought of walking all
the way to the square made me feel
very sleepy. I couldn't see Prissy

73

anywhere, so I closed my eyes again and fell into a deep sleep. Suddenly, a flood of icy water slooshed over me, drenching my fur, making me shiver and quiver.

I looked up, terrified, and there

was Prissy with a watering can in her hand and a nasty little smirk on her face. I hissed loudly, spat at her, and shook myself. If there's one thing I cannot bear, it's being damp in any way. Once, when I was a tiny kitten, I fell into a sink full of dishwater, and I have had a fear of wetness ever since. I began to walk toward her.

"Prissy, you beast," Miles shouted. "Look what you've done to Blossom. You're so horrible! You're the most horrible person I've ever met and I wish you'd never come to stay! I wish you'd go away!"

"She jumped on my bed!" Prissy whined. "She scared me, so there! Serves her right."

"Give me that watering can,"
Miles yelled, and he pulled it out of
Prissy's hand. Then he ran to
comfort me, just as Mum and Dad
burst out through the French doors
to see what all the noise was about.

"It's Miles," Prissy whined. "It's him. He's poured water on Blossom and he says I did! Look, he's holding the watering can."

"I took it away from her," Miles said. "She would have watered poor Blossom again. You know I wouldn't hurt her."

Prissy burst into tears.

"Now, now, Prissy," said Mum. "Stop crying. It couldn't have been Miles, so it must have been an accident. Did you mean to water the flowers and get Blossom instead?"

"Yes," said Prissy. "Blossom was in the way."

Mum said to Miles, "Take Blossom inside and dry her with a

kitchen towel. Now, Prissy, stop crying. We'll go and find you some lovely ice cream and chocolate sauce. You'd like that, wouldn't you, petal?"

They disappeared into the house, and Miles picked me up and took me to the garage.

"What do you think we can do, Blossom, to make Auntie Iris and Uncle Cliff take her away? Mum and Dad don't think there's anything wrong with her."

I purred at him, and because he understands exactly what all my sounds mean, he knew I was saying "We'll think of something, don't worry."

Geejay was in the square later that evening when I went for a stroll. I told him what had happened.

"I think," said Geejay, "that drastic action is called for. I think I can help you, Blossom. I know something that most humans hate and run away from."

"Tell me," I said. He whispered in my ear.

When I heard what Geejay was planning, I began to plot my revenge. Prissy would scream, I was quite sure. I couldn't wait for her to catch sight of the surprise that Geejay and I had in store for her.

5.
Goodbye, Prissy!

Sunday was even hotter than
Saturday. Perkins, Callie, and I had
found a spot in the heart of a
rhododendron bush where the sun
couldn't reach us, and we were lying
there asleep because the weather
was unsuitable for lively
conversation. There was no sign of
Geejay. I think I might have stayed

there all day, but my hunger got the better of me. It always does, especially on Sundays, when Mum makes delicious roasts for lunch.

"Goodbye," I said to my friends. "It's lamb today, I think."

"My people," said Perkins, "are having salad. It is fortunate that I am not much interested in food."

"He's a fussy eater," Callie whispered to me.

I made my way into my own garden.

"Psst!" whispered a familiar voice. It was Geejay. "Here I am, Blossom."

"Hello, Geejay. Have you got one?"

"Of course," said Geejay. "Here he is. A perfect little mouse with not a mark on him. Just one gentle swipe of my paw and he was out for the count."

"Thank you," I said. "You're a most excellent hunter, Geejay. I don't know what I'd do without you."

"It's a pleasure," said Geejay, and went off through the fence at the bottom of our garden.

I am not a good hunter. The thought of chasing things makes me feel tired. The Randalls have been excellent providers of food for years and years, and I've never been a cat to go tearing through the grass and bushes after small creatures who always manage to run faster than I do. I can't see the point of getting my paws muddy and my fur ruffled for something that's no more than a snack. I pushed Geejay's mouse from one paw to the other for a while, and he lay about looking as dead . . . well, as dead as an exceedingly dead mouse. I could smell the lamb cooking and I felt hungrier than ever. For a moment or two, I wondered where I could put my prey so that Prissy would see him and be scared out of her wits. I hoped this mouse would be the last straw and persuade our visitor that she didn't want to stay with us any longer.

Dad and Miles and Prissy were sitting at the table. I could see them from the kitchen door. Mum was getting ready to pass food through the hatch from the kitchen to the dining room. She was busy slicing lamb and arranging it on white plates. Next to the lamb, she put some round scoops of mashed potato and some green beans.

"Come and get these, dear," she called to Dad.

I knew which of the plates was Prissy's. Nobody was looking at me. I moved more quickly than I had done for a long time and dropped the dead mouse into the little valley between two mashed potato mountains. I had a daydream about what would happen . . . Prissy would lift the mouse to her lips with her fork, and possibly even bite on it

before she knew what she was
doing . . .

"There you are, Prissy," said Dad.
"This plate's for you."

"I like mashed potato," she said.
"It's my best thing."

"There you are, then," said Dad.
"Look, I'll put some gravy on it for
you. You like gravy, don't you?"

He didn't wait for an answer, but picked up the gravy boat and poured thick, brown liquid all over Prissy's lunch. It ran down the sides of the potatoes and formed a puddle on the plate.

Prissy dug her fork into the potato and lifted it to her mouth.

Either the gravy had magical powers, or the hidden rodent was not as dead as I had thought at first. Whiskers all a-twitch, he sat up on the fork and shook his head. He had a little spot of potato on his nose and his fur was damp with gravy. He took one look at Prissy and jumped down onto the plate. He scrambled over a pile of green beans and began to paddle in the gravy,

bending down to sip it every now
and then, and looking perkier than
any mouse I'd ever seen.

Prissy shrieked. She shrieked so
loudly that a cup fell off its hook on
the kitchen cupboard.

"Mouse! Look, Auntiee!"

Mum came running through from
the kitchen. Prissy leaped from her
chair and sent it flying. She knocked
her plate to the floor as well and
bumped into Mum, who just
happened to have Miles's lunch in

her hand. Lamb and potatoes and
beans soared into the air and slid
down the walls. Dad leaped from his
chair. It fell over backward and very
nearly squashed me flat as I was
running for the shelter of the
sideboard. The mouse flew up and
up and landed on the mantelpiece,

where he scattered all the bric-a-
brac onto the floor. They smashed
into a thousand fragments.

"Oh," cried Mum. "My treasures!"

"Calm down, Prissy," said Dad,
trying to sound firm. "It's only a

very little mouse. Look, I've caught it now and I'm going to take it to the garden. We'll get you another helping. I can't think where it came from. You're not a hunter, are you, Blossom? Blossom, where have you gone?"

I poked my head out of my hiding place and meowed.

"There she is," said Miles, and he winked at me. He was trying very hard not to laugh.

Prissy was the color of a beet and damp about the face. "I want my mummee!" she moaned, and whatever anyone said to her, she wouldn't be cheered up.

After ten minutes or so, we heard them. The words that Miles and I had been waiting for were spoken at long last.

"I want to go home! I don't want to stay here any longer!"

Mum said (rather quickly, I thought. Could it be she was tiring of darling little Prissy?), "Come on, then, dear, we'll go and phone your parents, though I don't know what Iris will say . . ."

The room looked as though a
small bomb had gone off in it. There
wasn't anywhere comfortable for a
cat to sit, so I went back to the
square.

"You did it, Blossom!" said Callie.
We had just watched the roaring car
tear out of the square, carrying
Prissy away with it.

Auntie Iris had arrived within
hours and piled the trunk full of her
daughter's belongings.

"Were Mum and Dad sorry to see
her go?" Perkins asked.

"They made sorry noises," I told
them, "but I know Mum was happy
to have everything calm again. It
was the bric-a-brac that did it, I

think. Mum is very fond of all her things. I think she would have made more of an effort to cheer Prissy up if they hadn't been broken."

"I knew the mouse trick would work," said Geejay. "Humans don't seem to like them at all. I can't think why. I find them delicious. My mouth waters when I think of mouse and mash!"

"Thank you, Geejay," I said. "And thanks to you, too, Perkins and Callie, for all your help. I must go and find Miles now. We are going to celebrate."

I found Miles in his room. He was sitting up in bed.

"I've got my room back," he said, patting the quilt. "But I've been waiting for you. Come on, jump up here."

I looked at him and blinked.

"Sorry, Bloss," he said. "I know you hate jumping. I'll pick you up."

He lifted me up gently. The quilt was squashy and warm, and I began to tread myself a lovely, soft nest in it, right next to Miles's legs.

"I like my bed," he said, "better than any other bed in the world."

"Especially with me curled up on it," I purred.

Miles understood exactly what I was saying. I know that, because he said the very same thing. "Especially with you curled up on it, Blossom."

I closed my eyes. Tomorrow would be a wonderfully peaceful, quiet day. I could feel it in my whiskers.

THE END

Picasso Perkins

1.
The Painting Competition

My name is Perkins and I am an old cat and a wise cat. I am, in addition, familiar with all the sayings of Our Ancient Furry Ancestors. They say, for instance, "Breakfast is the right meal for interesting news."

Today at breakfast, Lexie said: "Guess what? There's a painting competition in the *Bugle*. It's called

Paint Your Pet, and there are cash prizes! Also, the winning picture gets printed in the paper."

"Lovely, dear," said Melissa. "Please eat your cereal."

Lexie continued, through a spoonful of food, "Entries have to be in on Monday. I wish I'd known about this before . . . we haven't got enough time. I want to do a portrait

of Perkins. Jess'll be here in a second
and I'll tell her about it, and we'll
do it together. It's sure to win.
Perkins is so beautiful, aren't you,
Perkins?"

I looked up and blinked at her to
show her my gratitude. Little did I
know what I was letting myself in
for. Lexie likes to get her own way.
She is not a calm and docile child.
She goes upstairs two at a time; she
never walks when she can run; and
she climbs trees as well as many cats.

The Jess she was expecting is her best friend and she lives next door to us. Lexie is a great talker, just like her mother. Melissa is a teacher at Lexie's school and believes in recycling and the creative use of various foodstuffs. The children in her class are forever making sculptures from old cornflakes boxes and egg cartons, and sticking lentils, beans, and uncooked macaroni onto cardboard, spraying them with gold and silver paint, and taking them home to proud parents.

Roland Blythe, Lexie's father, is an artist.

"I'm a pro," he says. "A real professional. There's not many who can say they make a decent living from their brushes. Starving in a garret wouldn't suit us, eh?" he says to his wife and daughter.

Nevertheless, Roland would love to have his paintings exhibited in a proper art gallery. That is what he would call success. His pictures end up on greeting cards, calendars, and wrapping paper. Still, I know he has been preparing what he calls "real pictures" in a shed at the end of the garden, which he calls "my studio." It is a delightful, warm place to curl up in during the chilly months of the year, and Roland likes to chat to me as he works.

"I value your opinion, Perkins," he says to me. "Tell me what you think of this. I call it 'Seagulls at Sunset.'" He likes painting animals and birds. He has done "Puppies at Playtime," "Fluffy Fun" (rabbits), and "Purrfect Peace" (kittens asleep). I never tell Roland my opinion of his work, but Blossom, Callie, and Geejay know that I am not a great admirer of his pictures. Their colors are too bright or too pale. They are all much the same as one another and they are what Lexie and Jess call "soppy." Whenever Roland shows me something new, I purr enthusiastically and pretend to examine the painting carefully, but often my eyes are half-closed and I

am thinking about my next sleep and where I might be most comfortable. I would not wish to hurt his feelings, for as the Furry Ancestors say: "A purring cat is never short of chopped chicken liver." But let me return to the breakfast table. Lexie had decided my portrait was going to win a prize.

"That's very exciting, Lexie," said Roland, "but I have some thrilling news of my own. Look at this letter."

He waved it around, narrowly
missing the milk jug. "Wilfred de
Crespay is coming to view my work
on Saturday. That's tomorrow . . .
oh, my word!" He began to fan
himself with the letter. "I've gone
quite hot and bothered."

"Who's Wilfred the Crispy?" Lexie
said. "Is he foreign?"

"De Crespay," said Roland. "His name is probably of Norman origin, but he is English. He is one of the best-known art dealers in town. He goes to see what artists are painting and chooses pictures to go in his gallery. Then rich people buy them for lots and lots of money. I could be famous! I wrote to him some time ago but never really expected an answer. Goodness me! And such short notice! He says he likes to catch painters as they are and not give them too much time to prepare new work. But I must go and begin to get everything into a fit state to be seen."

When Roland is arranging paintings, it is as well to avoid his studio. He picks things up and puts them down somewhere else. He takes three steps backward to look at something, and if I happen to be in the way, my tail is almost certain to be trodden on. So I decided to settle down in Lexie's room. Lexie is an excellent child in many ways, but no one would call her tidy. Her bedroom looks as though a medium-sized hurricane has lifted every garment, every book, and every knickknack, whirled them around in the air for a time, and put them down in unexpected places.

It is quite normal
to find a sneaker on
the windowsill,

 or a book
on the
pillow,

or a pair of socks
draped over the
dressing-table mirror.
Still, she is always glad
to see me and there is
generally a space on the bed into
which I can fit myself if I curl up
really small. Sometimes good luck is
with me and one of Lexie's
cardigans is spread out and waiting
for me.

"Perkins!" she cried, following me
as I edged my way into the room.
"I'm going to paint the best picture
of you ever. And Jess is going to help
me."

Jess had already arrived at our
house, waiting to walk to school
with Lexie. She said, "You'll like
having your portrait done, won't
you, Perkins? If we win, your picture
will be in the paper. It's going to be
brilliant."

"And," Lexie said, "we're not going to do the normal cat things. We're not going to show you sleeping or looking cute or anything. It's going to be dead unusual."

I have never thought of myself as cute, but I did not say anything.

"We'll think," Lexie continued, "of good places for you to sit."

"Or stand," said Jess.

"Or maybe lie," said Lexie. "You'll have to keep very still. You can do that, can't you, Perkins? You're often still for ages, just staring into space."

I jumped onto Lexie's bed and decided to ignore her last remark. Many humans think that cats stare into space, but we do not. We are

thinking cat thoughts (for example:
Do the sounds from the kitchen
mean that Melissa is cooking, and if
she is, will there be scraps for me?),
dreaming cat dreams, and seeing cat
things invisible to the human eye,
such as specks of flying dust drifting
through the air and catching the
light.

"We'll use pastel crayons," said Lexie.

"No, watercolors," said Jess. "I want to use my new paint box."

"Okay," said Lexie. "We'll try watercolors, but maybe we should do some sketches first. There are a few minutes before we have to go to school. My dad always does sketches."

It occurred to me that sketching had not done much to improve Roland's pictures, but I kept quiet and hoped the girls would be content to draw me as I lay on the bed.

Not a bit of it. Lexie picked me up and said, "Now, stand here, Perkins, and try to look fierce!"

She deposited me on top of the bookshelf, and fierce is just what I felt, so I glowered at her. The Furry Ancestors say: "Better wide awake than being woken up," and it is true that I intensely dislike being interrupted as I am falling asleep, so I went on glowering.

"That's lovely!" Lexie squeaked. "Now don't move while we draw you."

She and Jess began to scratch around on sheets of paper. The top of the bookshelf was covered with bits and pieces: jewelry, pencils, ornaments, and so forth, and there wasn't an inch of space where a cat could put his feet. So I jumped down onto the carpet and ran out of the room.

"Perkins!" Lexie shouted. "Come back here at once! Naughty cat!"

She tore down the stairs behind me and very nearly caught me, but even at my advanced age, I am quite nippy on my feet in an emergency, and thankfully, Lexie cannot follow me through the cat-flap. I made my way to the garden in the middle of the square.

2.
Hiding from Lexie

"Please do not let her find me," I said to my friends. "I am staying here under this bush and I am not coming out till Lexie and Jess have left for school."

The other Cuckoo Square Cats stared at me in some amazement. If there is one thing they all know, it is how fond I am of Lexie and how devoted she is to me.

I am the oldest cat in the square. I came here with Roland and Melissa Blythe when they first moved into number 27, thirteen years ago. In those days I was a sweet, fluffy kitten and so good-tempered and loving that I was called Purrkins. But the Furry Ancestors say: "The name must grow with the cat," so I have become Perkins. Lexie's real name is Alexandra. She is eight years old. My closest companions

among the neighborhood cats are
Blossom,

Callie,

and Geejay.
They look up to me, and I find that
I can often give them good advice. I
enjoy sitting with them in the little
garden in the middle of Cuckoo

Square. We tell one another stories about the humans who feed and shelter us and amuse us greatly with their strange behavior.

"Your family," Callie said to me one day, "is stranger than most."

"That's because," said Blossom, "Mr. Blythe is an artist. It's a well-known fact that artistic people are not like everyone else. For one thing, they wear funny clothes. Think of Mr. Blythe's beret."

This is made of black velvet, and we cats smile every time we see it.

"He calls it his Rembrandt beret," I told my friends. "Rembrandt was a famous artist who lived long ago."

"Is Mr. Blythe famous?" Geejay wanted to know.

"Not really," I told them, "though he would love to be."

I am grateful that I do not have to wear strange garments. I am proud of the glossiness of my tabby fur, of the youthful sparkle in my amber eyes, and of my imposing size, but I am a modest cat, so I try never to mention these things.

"Look!" said Callie. "There's Lexie going off to school with Jess."

"They are never apart," I told her. "Any room that Lexie is in will contain Jess and vice versa. And

now, they will be spending most of
the time in our house, because of
me. They are after me. That is why I
am hiding. Lexie was going to start
the project that very minute."

"What project, Perkins?" Geejay
asked. "All we know is that Lexie is
after you, but we don't know why."

"Did I not mention why?"

"No," said Blossom. "You didn't."

127

"Lexie is going to paint my portrait. There is a competition in the newspaper, and she intends to win it. She has just tried to get me to stand very still exactly where she wants me, and it was most uncomfortable, I can tell you. I would much rather it did not happen again, and therefore I have decided to hide in the square when she is at home. If she cannot find me, then she will not be able to pull me about this way and that. While Lexie is at school, I shall be warm and comfortable in the house, and when she returns I shall come out here."

"But it's getting so cold here in the evenings," said Callie. "And the bangs have started. I heard some last night."

We all shuddered. Every leaf on the trees in the square was turning red or gold or brown and spiraling down to make a wonderfully crackly sitting spot for us cats, but November means Guy Fawkes Night, when children set off fireworks. We hide in the darkest spaces we can find until the fizzings and the whizzings of a thousand exploding missiles are over.

The Furry Ancestors say: "When fire leaps in the sky, sensible cats hide in the nearest cupboard."

"I shall be brave," I said. "It is only for a few days. The entries for the competition have to be in on Monday, and today is Friday. I will say goodbye to you all now and go in for a sleep on my special shawl. Have I told you that Melissa has put out a beautifully striped, soft, hand-knitted shawl just for me?"

"Often," said Geejay. "You've often told us."

I meowed a farewell to my friends and made my way home. I pushed myself through the cat-flap—a tight fit these days—and into the kitchen.

3.
Posing for the Portrait

I looked all around the kitchen to make sure Roland was not in there, using his horrible hissing coffee machine to make himself a drink. A blissful silence filled every corner of the room. I jumped onto my special chair and began my morning wash. First I cleaned my face, then I licked my front paws, and then I tackled

the hard-to-reach bit of my back,
thinking what a fortunate feline I
was to have such a beautifully soft,
stripy shawl to lie on. Then I put my
face between my paws and fell into
a deep slumber. I do not know how
long I had been sleeping when I
heard the sound of a key opening
the front door.

"Coo-ee!" called Melissa.
"Roland, dear, are you there?"

"Dad!" shouted Lexie. "It's us.
Where are you?"

"I was in the box room a moment ago," said Roland. "I was looking for some frames. I've nearly decided what to show Mr. de Crespay tomorrow. What are you doing here?"

"We've been sent home from school," said Lexie. "The boiler's broken and it won't be fixed till after the weekend. Isn't that ace?" She was bouncing up and down. "Jess is coming over," she continued, "and we'll do the portrait. We can spend all day on it, can't we, Perkins?"

I had tucked my head firmly under my paws and was busily pretending to be still asleep.

Lexie was not deceived. "You're awake, Perkins," she said, stroking me. "I know you are. I can tell because your tail is twitching. And," she went on, "don't even think about running off to the square or even the studio because I shan't let you."

She put the cat-flap cover on, and

my whiskers quivered with indignation.

"When Jess comes," she said to Melissa, "send her up to the box room to help me bring paper down."

"How much paper are you going to need?" Melissa asked. "You can only send one picture in, you know."

"We might," said Lexie, "need a few sheets to practice on, till we get it right. That's okay, isn't it?"

"It's fine," said Melissa. "Just leave everything tidy in there, that's all."

The box room is called that because it is full of boxes: the packages and egg cartons and yogurt pots and toilet paper rolls that Melissa uses to make things with her children at school. There is

also a cupboard in there where the
paper lives. Melissa's brother, Uncle
Don, works with a machine that
spits out yards and yards of it every
day. He calls the machine a
computer, and he brings his sister
piles and piles of clean white paper,
which everyone uses for drawing
and painting.

Lexie was in the box room for a
long time, and when she returned to
the kitchen, she whispered to me:

"Don't say a word, Perkins, but this isn't computer printout. I've taken some of Dad's real paper. Otherwise the pictures are going to look babyish, don't you think?"

I thought to myself that Roland might be extremely angry when he discovered that Lexie was helping herself to his possessions, but Lexie said, "He won't even notice it's gone, he's in such a state about Wilfred the Scrumpy."

Jess arrived soon after, and then the torment began.

"Now, Perkins, stand up," said Lexie. I ignored her. She and Jess were sitting at the kitchen table. They each had a jam jar full of water, and a paint box in front of them, and also a big sheet of paper for the picture.

"He's going to be difficult," said
Lexie. "I'll go and get him to stand
up." She picked me up and shook
me gently. Then she put me down
on all four paws. "There," she said.
"Now stay like that and don't move.
Try and look like a statue."

I obliged her for a moment, but I
sat down on my haunches after a
while.

"Perkins!" Lexie shrieked. "What are you doing? Silly cat!"

"He looks all right," said Jess. "Let's do him like that. He still looks quite fierce."

I glanced at the kitchen door and noticed that Melissa had not closed it behind her. The Furry Ancestors would have been proud of me. I recalled one of their best-known sayings: "The open door waits for the fleeing cat," and before Lexie could say "Jam jar," I had streaked through it and bounded upstairs.

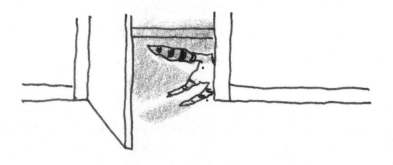

"Perkins!" I heard the girls calling after me, and soon they were thumping up the stairs behind me. I ran into Roland and Melissa's bedroom and dived under the comforter, making myself as flat as I possibly could, because everyone knows the ancient saying: "A flat cat is a safe cat, a flatter cat is a safer cat, and the flattest cat is the safest cat of all."

"I can see you," Lexie cried. "There's a big lump in the middle of the bed—that's you, Perkins, and I'm coming to get you!"

It is one thing to know a saying by heart and quite another to be able to obey it. I sighed. It was clear that I would never be nearly flat enough to escape Lexie's sharp eyes. Still, I was not going to let the girls crawl under the comforter to find me. That would have been most undignified. I made my own way out, trying to look as though I did not at all mind being found and carried back to the kitchen.

As soon as she had settled me where she thought I ought to be, Lexie shut the door very firmly and said, "Let's start again, then."

The sheets of paper fell off the table like leaves from the trees outside. The portrait would not come right.

"His head's too big," said Jess after one attempt.

"Now his paws look funny," said Lexie, throwing another sheet of paper onto the floor.

"And I don't think he should sit like that," she added, tossing the next bit of paper aside. "Let's move him."

I sighed. No sooner was I placed in one position than the girls decided they wanted me somewhere else, and they moved me around the kitchen until I felt quite dizzy. First they put me on the sideboard.

Then they put me
beside the door.

Then they tried me
on the windowsill,
and the pile of rejected portraits
grew and grew until the whole floor
was covered with white, paint-
streaked sheets.

"Girls!" Melissa said when she came into the kitchen to cook the supper. "What have you been doing?"

"It's Perkins's fault," said Jess. "He keeps moving. We can't get it right."

"He's a cat," said Lexie. "He's never been an artist's model. He'll be better next time, now that he's used to it."

I groaned.

Melissa said, "Well, I can't have this mess everywhere. Wilfred de Crespay is coming to lunch tomorrow, and I haven't even started on the quiche."

"Wilfred the Crunchy!" said Lexie, and she and Jess began to giggle.

"Stop being silly, girls," said Melissa, "and please take any paper you don't want to the studio, and leave it in a neat pile on the shelf there. I'll take any sheets you decide you've finished with to school when we go back. I can use it for some papier-mâché masks we're making."

Lexie and Jess, still snorting with laughter, gathered up armfuls of paper and made their way to the studio.

"Poor old Perkins," said Melissa. "Off you go to the square, then. You've been very patient."

Geejay was the only cat I could find to talk to. He said, "Blossom and Callie have gone back to their houses. I don't suppose they will be out again tonight."

"After the afternoon I've had," I told him, "I shall make sure I spend most of this evening and tomorrow under this very bush. I have not had a moment's peace."

"Poor old you," said Geejay.

I appreciated his sympathy, and I thought I had worked out a perfect way of avoiding Lexie, but I did not know then about the storm blowing through the sky on its way toward us, which would change every one of my plans.

4.

In the Studio

The storm was one of the fiercest I had ever seen. I was forced to leave the square and come inside much earlier than I had intended, but mercifully, Lexie had already gone to sleep. Gales battered the trees and shook the windows in their frames all night long, and sleet fell from the sky like little gray needles. By the

time morning came, the storm had
stopped being quite so stormy, but
rain was pouring down the panes
of the kitchen window, and the
wind was still rattling the cat-flap.
This was an indoors day if ever
there was one. Not even Geejay,
who is the bravest of us all, would
venture out on a morning like this.

As the Furry Ancestors say: "Warm and dry is better than wet and cold." Before the Blythes woke up, I worried about a hiding place. Lexie knew all my secret cupboards and quiet spots, and she and Jess intended to spend the morning working on their portrait of me. They had said so yesterday. It was Roland who came to my rescue.

"I've got everything set up in the studio," he announced at breakfast, "and I don't want anyone—*anyone at all*, Lexie, do you understand?—coming in there and spoiling all my hard work. I've touched up a few of the pictures, so some of the paint isn't even quite dry. Out of bounds, okay?"

"Okay, Dad," said Lexie, attacking her toast with a buttery knife. "Precious Mr. Wilfred the Munchy will see them all just as you've arranged them. I'm going to be busy anyway. We've got to finish our entry for the competition."

I jumped down from the chair and made my way over to the cat-flap. I would have to sneak out as quietly as I could and then cross the muddy, dripping garden, but it would be worth it. A whole morning till lunchtime in a place that Lexie had been forbidden to visit—what could be better? I chose my moment carefully. Lexie and her mother were in the middle of a loud and extremely boring argument about whether or not Lexie needed a new pair of jeans. I edged my way over to the cat-flap and pushed at it with my nose. A blast of icy air containing far too much wetness to be comfortable blew right up my nostrils.

"Courage, Perkins!" I said to
myself. "Remember—Lexie and Jess
will never find you. Onward!"

Out into the garden I went, and I
do not think I have ever crossed it so
fast. Sodden leaves fluttered around
my paws, sharp winds puffed at my
fur, and rain seemed to be coming at
me from all directions. I knew the
studio would be shut, but I had my

secret door that no one knew about. There was a small gap between the planks of one wall, right at the bottom, and I would have to squeeze through that. I remembered the saying: "The closed portal invites the furry paw," and I did it, but not without a great deal of difficulty. I am larger than I thought I was, and by the time I had forced my way in, I felt as though I'd been stretched and squashed into a sort of snake shape.

The studio was not as warm as when Roland was in it with his heater on, but after the horrors of the garden, it seemed very pleasant. I shook myself and licked myself clean, and looked around to see where I could sleep. Roland's paintings were standing up all over the room, and the big pile of Lexie and Jess's used paper sat tidily on the first shelf. I nosed around in the corners, and by a wonderful stroke of luck I discovered in one of them an old sweater that Roland had forgotten to pick up.

"Perfect, Perkins, just the ticket!" I said, and began to settle myself in the woolly bed I had found. I suppose I must have fallen asleep at once. Running so fast first thing in the morning and then squeezing through such a tiny gap had exhausted me.

Then a particularly strong wind came along and blew the studio door open. Roland must have forgotten to lock it. It is not quite true to say I woke up. The noise was such a shock that I leaped into the air with every separate hair of my fur standing on end. The gale now blowing into the studio lifted Lexie and Jess's pieces of paper right off the shelf and spread them out all over the floor. It also knocked over a small vase of flowers that Roland was in the middle of painting, and

the water made a puddle around the
easel, which had been set up near
the window.

No sooner had the gale opened
the door than another gust
appeared and slammed it shut
again. I waited to see whether the
wind had decided to leave the studio
alone for a while, and then I went
to investigate the puddle. I am very
fond of puddles. Indeed, I enjoy
them as much as any cat I know,
and I had a lovely time for a while,
dipping my paws and licking the
edges of the water.

Then I did something I should never have done. I leaped up onto the shelf where Roland keeps his paints. I heard voices and took fright. I thought Lexie might be disobeying her father and coming to find me. It turned out to be the neighbors, talking about the damage the storm had done in their garden. The shelf is narrow, and I landed very precisely on top of Roland's paint box, which he had left open. Each of my paws was now covered with a different color. The paint was powdery, and I disliked most intensely the way it smelled and the way it felt.

"The puddle, Perkins!" I said to myself. "Remember what the Furry

Ancestors advise: 'Paddle in a puddle for perfect paw hygiene.'"

This worked well. I walked backward and forward across the girls' pictures lying on the floor, and my paws dried very nicely. At first I left colorful tracks on the paper, but these grew paler and paler, and at last I considered my paws clean

enough to lick. I was wondering whether to do them now or wait until I had made my way back to the house, when I heard Roland's voice saying, "This way, Mr. de Crespay, please follow me," and then another, higher voice saying, "Oh, do call me Wilfred, I beseech you! De Crespay is too, too formal, don't you think?"

I shot away and hid behind a rather large canvas that was leaning against one wall. The whole family had come to the studio with this distinguished visitor. I peeped out to get a good look at him. He was tall and spaghetti-thin and he wore a long purple velvet jacket and green boots.

Lexie and Jess were standing very close to me, and I could hear them whispering and trying not to giggle.

"Call me the Chewy!" Jess breathed.

"No, no," Lexie murmured. "That's too, too formal. Just Chewy, please!"

Wilfred was silent for a long time. The mess before his eyes was clearly not quite what he was expecting, but he took a deep breath and began to peer at everything. Then he sighed. Roland followed him about anxiously, also somewhat puzzled at the state of his studio. Melissa was frowning. She could see that Roland was worried. The famous art dealer hummed to

himself. Then he bent down and began to pick up all the sheets of paper I had walked over.

"This," he said. "This is very different from most of your work, Roland. Perhaps it's a new departure, and I must say, I am somewhat dazzled by its sheer beauty and elegance. Look at these delicate traceries of color! Look at the truth of the line—oh, it's in the spirit of the great Japanese masters—you really have found yourself, dear chap, haven't you? The Americans will be thrilled to ribbons, trust me, my dear—yes, yes, I think we will all, in the words of someone or other, clean up, and laugh all the way to the bank!"

"But," said Roland, blushing, "Mr. de Crespay . . ."

"Wilfred," said Wilfred, "I implore you!"

"Sorry . . . Wilfred . . . well, these are not my work."

"Not your work? Whatever can you mean? You don't suppose . . ." He looked at Lexie and Jess and winked at them. "You don't suppose he has an army of elves that comes and paints these masterpieces while he's asleep, do you?"

"No," said Lexie. "He doesn't. Those look like the pictures Jess and I did yesterday. This is Jess." She pushed Jess forward. "But ours didn't have those colored bits there. I don't know how those could

possibly have got there."

Wilfred looked at the girls, then back at the paintings. "Extraordinary! I don't know what to call them . . . They are *visions!*"

"They weren't meant to be visions," said Lexie. "They're supposed to be portraits of Perkins. Perkins is our cat."

"Well, I'm lost for words!" said Wilfred. "I don't know when I've seen such work, and now there is a mystery surrounding their creation."

Lexie looked at Jess and Jess looked at Lexie.

"Who could have done that to our papers?" said Jess. "Perhaps there's a phantom painter who breaks into people's sheds and changes stuff."

"Studio," said Roland. "Not 'shed,' please, Jess—and I'm sure there must be some kind of reasonable explanation."

I decided that this was the moment to let everyone see me, so I came out from behind the canvas that was hiding me and walked

across one of the pictures. It seemed
that my puddle-dipping had not
been very successful, because I left a
trail of pale pink paw prints behind
me.

"It's Perkins!" Lexie shouted. "That's him, and he's the one who made the marks on the paper."

"Goodness!" said Wilfred. "That is truly amazing—an artistic cat! Ooh, you're a real beauty!" he said to me, and to Lexie and Jess he said, "Of course, the marks had to be made by a real cat. I can see it all now! They absolutely make the works so true, so very authentically feline! They will fit perfectly into an exhibition I am planning. I am calling it 'The Face of Nature,' and these cat portraits will fit in most beautifully. The show will be mainly landscapes, of course, but these, with Perkins's own inimitable finishing touches, will be the talk of the art world. No one will be able to resist them. I shall be in touch with the press at once."

"What about," said Roland, "my work?" He was looking a little sad, I thought.

"Oh, divine, divine, dear chap, but not quite what I'm looking for . . . not quite *natural* enough, don't you see? I shall, however, pass your name on to one of my colleagues. I think your style is just what he may be looking for."

He swept out of the studio, and Lexie and Jess and Melissa followed him.

"I don't suppose," Roland said to me, "you'd consider taking a short walk across one of my paintings,

Perkins, old chap? It might turn it
into an instant masterpiece."

I fled, most eager to tell my
friends in the square what had
happened, and certainly *not* wanting
to dip my feet into any horrible
colors ever again.

5.
A Change of Plan

"Are you famous now, Perkins?"
Blossom asked me, later on Saturday
afternoon. The storm had subsided,
the sun was shining, and the sky was
now a delicious pale blue.

"Perhaps not quite yet," I said,
"but I very soon will be. Mr. de
Crespay has arranged for a
photographer to come and take

pictures of Lexie and Jess and myself. Of course, I will not mind that nearly as much as sitting for my portrait, because, as you know, photographs are taken so quickly. To tell you the truth, I am quite looking forward to it."

"Perhaps," said Callie wistfully, "they'll come and take a picture of you in the square with us."

"But what about the competition?" said Geejay. "What will the girls send in now?"

I had not thought of that. I sighed. "I suppose I ought to go in and allow them to paint me again if they want to," I said. "It would hardly be fair to spoil their plans. I shall come out and see you all later."

The girls had changed their minds. When I arrived in the kitchen, they were nowhere to be seen.

"Hello, Perkins!" said Melissa. "Mr. de Crespay has just left. Isn't it all exciting? You are a clever cat! And the girls—aren't they talented? Mr. de Crespay—I must remember to call him Wilfred—says their youthful high spirits come out in the pictures. I wonder if I have time to get my hair done before that photographer comes tomorrow. Do you want to know where the girls are? They're over at Jess's."

I was relieved to be allowed to sleep peacefully, but still I wished that Lexie and Jess had decided to stay at our house. Had they made up their minds not to enter the competition? And if they still wished to compete, how could they paint my portrait if I was not there? I fretted about this for some time, but in the end my eyes closed and I slept. In the wise words of the Furry Ancestors: "Sleep makes everything bearable."

"Perkins! Perkins, wake up!"

It was Lexie. She was standing beside my shawl, waving a sheet of paper in front of me. "Look at this! Isn't it great?"

I looked. It was a painting of a fish in a bowl.

"This is Jess's fish. He's called Harold. We painted him this afternoon, and we're sending his picture in to the newspaper, for the competition."

I felt a pang of jealousy, I admit it, and Lexie evidently read my mind.

"You mustn't be jealous, Perkins. You're going to be properly famous. Your pictures are going to hang in a proper gallery, and there's going to be a photo of you in the local

paper. So it's only fair that Jess's pet
has his picture painted. Isn't it?"

I had to confess that it was.

6.
Fame!

If you have never been famous,
permit me to tell you that it is
extremely tiring. I am not the only
cat in the square to say this.
Blossom and Callie and Geejay
shared some of my limelight, and
we all waited with some excitement
for the newspaper to appear the
next day.

While he was with us, the man with the camera never stopped talking to me. He walked around me flashing shiny lights in my eyes. He started in the house. Lexie had to cuddle me and put me on her lap, and then Jess had to do the same thing. After that, the girls had to

stand and smile stupidly at sheets of paper which were pretending to be the Perkins Paintings. They were not the real pictures, because Wilfred de Crespay had taken those off to be framed, ready to hang in his gallery.

"Kitty, kitty, kitty," the photographer kept saying, and "Over here, Pussycat . . ." and "How about a shot of you cleaning your whiskers?" and "Watch the birdy—you like watching birdies, don't you, eh?"

They took us all out to the square in the end, because the sun was shining. Blossom, Callie, and Geejay had been waiting by the fence.

"Where have you been, Perkins?" Blossom meowed at me as I went to stand beside her. "We'd given up hope."

"Fabulous shot!" the photographer screeched. "Don't move a muscle, cats! Three other cats . . . the Perkins fan club, I bet! Stand still, kitties."

The Cuckoo Square Cats were a success. We stood and sat and looked interesting for a long time, and then at last the photographer packed his camera away and left us alone.

"You are lovely cats," Lexie said. "And if you're in the paper tomorrow, I shall come out and show you the picture."

There were two pictures in the *Bugle* the next day. One was of Lexie and Jess sitting on a Cuckoo Square bench with myself in Lexie's arms, and Blossom, Callie, and Geejay gathered at the girls' feet. The other was a picture of Lexie and Jess with yours truly looking soulful in Lexie's arms. The caption

said, "Perkins, the Pussycat Picasso!"

I explained to my friends that Picasso was a famous painter, and I think they were impressed.

"I hope," said Geejay, "that you won't take to wearing a velvet beret like Mr. Blythe, now that you're an artist."

"Never," I said. "You know what the Furry Ancestors would say: 'East or West, fur is best.'"

You will be eager to know the results of the Paint Your Pet competition. The picture of Jess's goldfish won third prize. This is, I think you will agree, an excellent result for a creature who is not a cat.

THE END

About the Author

Adèle Geras has published more than seventy acclaimed books for children and young adults, including *My Grandmother's Stories,* which won the Sydney Taylor award in 1991. Her most recent novel is *Troy*. She is married, has two grown-up daughters, and lives in Manchester, England. She loves books, movies, all kinds of theater, and, of course, cats.

About the Illustrator

Tony Ross is the award-winning illustrator of several books for children, including the Amber Brown series by Paula Danziger. He lives with his family in Cheshire, England.